Published 1982 by Warwick Press,
730 Fifth Avenue, New York, New York 10019.

First published in Great Britain by
Kingfisher Books Limited, 1981.

Printed in Portugal by Gris Impressores
S.A.R.L., Cacém.

Library of Congress Catalog Card No. 81–51789

ISBN 0–531–09193–7

THE LAST JOURNEY

David Kent

Adviser:
Reverend Graham Mitchell

Illustrated by
Gwen Green, Francis Phillips
and Martin Reiner

WARWICK PRESS

Book 6: The Last Journey

THESE STORIES come from the last months of Jesus' life, and the years soon afterwards. His deeds of loving-kindness won Jesus many followers. But he could be stern too—at least with people who thought they understood God completely. So Jesus made enemies as well as friends. Powerful Jewish leaders, realizing what a threat he was to their idea of God, grew afraid of him. They managed to persuade the Roman rulers to put him to death.

But Jesus' death was not the end. The Bible tells us he rose from the dead and visited his followers, before he went at last to be with God. Then some of his followers began to talk about him, and to say what his life and death meant. And so Christianity began.

Simon Peter

Jesus loved all his disciples. Where he went they followed, helping to cure the sick, and to control the crowds that came to see Jesus.

But Jesus badly wanted to know what the disciples thought of him.

One day he asked his disciples, "Who do men say I am?"

They replied, "Some say you are John the Baptist; others say Elijah; others, Jeremiah or one of the prophets."

So people thought he might be one of God's dead but famous messengers come alive again.

Then Jesus asked them outright, "But who do *you* think I am?"

There was a short pause. Most of the disciples were not sure what to say. But Simon, who was also called Peter, had no doubts. "You are the Christ, the chosen one, the son of God," he declared.

Jesus smiled. "Bless you Simon," he said. "Only my Father in heaven can have told you that. Your other name, Peter, means 'rock' and I shall make you the rock on which I shall build my church. I shall give you the keys of the kingdom of heaven, with the power to lock or to open its doors."

Much later Peter traveled to Rome, and Roman Catholics believe he made that city the chief center of the Christian faith. This is why they see the pope—Peter's successor as bishop of Rome—as the leader of Christians everywhere.

Lazarus is Raised from the Dead

One of the many wonderful stories about Jesus tells how he brought a dead man back to life.

The story begins with bad news from the little town of Bethany. Martha and her sister Mary sent Jesus a message: "Lazarus, your friend and our brother, is very ill."

You might think Jesus would have hurried over to help. But fond as he was of Lazarus, he waited another two days. His reason will become plain in a moment.

At last he told his disciples he was ready to go. This worried them.

They said, "Only a few days back the Jewish leaders in that part of Palestine were trying to kill you."

Jesus seemed quite unconcerned for his safety. He said, "Lazarus is dead. I am glad I was not there when it happened—going now will give you fresh reasons for believing in me." So reluctantly they set out with Jesus for Bethany.

On the way they met Martha. Brushing tears from her eyes, she sobbed, "Lord, if you had been here he would still be alive."

But Jesus calmly told her, "Your brother will live again, for I bring the dead to life. Anyone who believes in me will live again—for ever—even though he seems to die like anyone else. Do you believe me Martha?"

"Yes, Lord," she said. "I believe you are the son of God, the messiah we have waited for."

Jesus stayed outside the village while Martha went home to fetch Mary. She returned with a group of Jewish leaders who had been consoling her. Seeing them all wailing and crying brought tears of pity to Jesus' eyes.

One Jewish leader murmured, "See how fond he was of Lazarus." But another said, "He made a blind man see—why didn't he save his own friend?"

At Lazarus' Tomb

Jesus asked where Lazarus was buried. Sadly they led him to the tomb where the dead man lay. It was a cave, closed by a huge stone.

"Roll the stone away", Jesus ordered. The people wondered what Jesus was going to do. After all, Lazarus had been dead four days.

Jesus spoke a short prayer. Then he cried, "Lazarus, come out!"

Something moved inside the darkness. Everyone shrank back with fright as a strange figure stepped out. It was a man, wrapped tightly in grave cloths from head to foot.

"Unbind him," Jesus commanded. Then everyone saw it was indeed Lazarus, back from the dead!

Many of the watching Jews now believed in Jesus' amazing powers. But the Jewish priests were afraid and jealous. They began to plan how to get rid of Jesus.

Jesus Enters Jerusalem

One spring day Jesus set out on his last great journey—a trip to celebrate the yearly Passover feast in the Jewish capital, Jerusalem. By now he was famous; thousands adored him. But Jewish priests in the city wanted him dead. He guessed his journey was risky, but he felt he must go just the same.

When Jesus neared Jerusalem he sent two disciples to a small village, saying, "Bring me the young donkey that you'll find tied up there. Say

your master must borrow it and will
bring it back soon."

They duly returned with the
animal, and threw their cloaks on its
back as a makeshift saddle.

Then Jesus mounted the donkey
and rode slowly up the steep, narrow
road leading into the city.

Meanwhile, news of his coming had spread. A huge crowd collected, and a great shout went up when the citizens saw Jesus approaching. People dashed into the road, dropping their coats for his donkey to walk on. Others strewed his path with a carpet of leafy palm branches.

All around him people were shouting, "Hail to the King! Blessed is he who comes in the Lord's name! Praise God for bringing back our father David's kingdom!"

It was a welcome fit for an emperor, for thousands believed that Jesus was not just a great religious teacher. They thought he was a new, powerful leader come to throw out their hated Roman rulers.

The Moneylenders

As soon as Jesus reached Jerusalem he entered the temple, Palestine's holiest building.

Like other religious buildings, the Jewish temple was built as a place of worship. Inside you would expect to find people kneeling quietly in prayer. Not in this temple, though.

As Jesus entered the building, he found what looked and sounded more like a market place than a temple. Rows of stalls were thronged with people, buying and selling all kinds of goods. Many were money changers; stalls where you could exchange one kind of money for another—for temple offerings could only be made in Jewish money. There were stalls, too, where traders sold doves and lambs. These were not bought as pets, but by worshipers who wanted to offer them as sacrifices to God.

Jesus' face went almost scarlet with rage when he saw all this, and realized that these merchants were just using the holy building as a way to make money. He decided to do something about it.

Next day, he strode back to the temple, and stormed inside. Then he furiously started overturning the stalls, scattering coins, doves and goods of all kinds. At the same time he began driving the buyers and sellers out onto the street.

Had he been anyone else they might have tried to fight back. But Jesus' rage so scared them that they just scrambled to save what they could, before scampering off.

They could not escape the lash of his tongue, though. Jesus shouted, "The Bible says God's temple is a place of prayer. You have turned it into a robbers' den!"

When he had thrown them all out of the temple, Jesus stayed there for a while, healing the sick.

All this made the chief priests look pretty silly. After all, they should not have allowed traders to misuse the temple. So the priests hated Jesus more than ever, and wished he had never shown up.

The Last Supper

Jesus' last days in Jerusalem were exciting but dangerous ones. People flocked to hear him preach, but Jesus had accused the temple priests of being proud, greedy and selfish. He was right and they knew it, and they hated him for it.

Each day Jesus preached, the danger grew. He knew the priests were scheming to kill him. Outside Jerusalem he might be safe, and so far he had stayed at a house on the edge of the city. But now he planned to celebrate the first evening of the Jewish Passover feast inside the city.

Somehow—the disciples never learned how—Jesus knew just where they would eat. He told two of them, "Go on ahead. Follow a man with a water pot to a house. Tell the person in charge you have come to see the room he has ready for us. He'll lead you upstairs to a large room set out for supper."

Discovery of a Traitor

The disciples found things just as Jesus had said they would.

That evening Jesus and the other disciples arrived, and all 13 of them sat down to eat. The table was laid simply with bowls, jugs of water and wine, and a dish of small, flat loaves of bread—hardly as much of a feast as most meals we enjoy.

The disciples were silent and uneasy. Now and then one glanced over his shoulder to make sure no enemies had crept in behind them.

Jesus solemnly studied their faces. He did not want to upset them, but he had something important to say.

Sadly he announced, "One of the twelve of you will betray me."

There was a shocked silence. Most of them could not believe it. But they knew Jesus had great insight into people's hearts. So one by one they asked, "Is it me?"

Jesus said nothing. Then a disciple called John asked outright, "Who is it, Lord?" Jesus replied, "It is the one to whom I give bread dipped in sauce," and he gave the bread to Simon Iscariot's son, named Judas.

Judas rushed out, but Jesus did not stop him. He said, "I have to die, just as the prophets foretold long ago." He felt that giving his life was making a sacrifice that would bring people closer to God.

No one much enjoyed the meal after that. But Jesus seemed as calm and relaxed as ever. He asked God to bless a loaf of bread, and thanked God for the wine. Then he handed bread and wine to his followers, saying, "Eat—this is my body. Drink —this is my blood."

Then he told them that when he was dead they must eat bread and drink wine in his memory. It was a meal none of them ever forgot.

The Garden of Gethsemane

All seemed peaceful that night as Jesus and his disciples left the supper room in Jerusalem, and walked toward their lodgings. But Jesus knew that his enemies were close and ready to strike.

Jesus told his disciples they would soon desert him. But Peter cried out angrily, "I'll never leave you!"

Jesus smiled knowingly and said, "Peter, three times tonight you will say you don't even know me."

They came to an old olive grove, and Jesus told his disciples to rest while he walked off alone to pray. It was quiet and beautiful here in the garden of Gethsemane, and moonlight shone through the trees.

Jesus felt suddenly afraid when he thought of the tortures and death in store for him. He prayed that God might let him escape all this pain. Yet in his heart he knew that his death was part of a plan to bring people nearer to God.

Kneeling down, he cried out to God, "Let your will be done!"

Meanwhile, his tired disciples had fallen asleep. All was silent. Suddenly there came a loud tramping of feet and a flashing of lights. The disciples awoke with a start, to see Judas leading a crowd of priests and soldiers into the olive grove, and straight towards Jesus!

Judas embraced Jesus as though they were still friends. But Jesus knew that this was an act of betrayal —perhaps for a reward of money, or perhaps because Jesus had not turned out to be the kind of leader that Judas had hoped for.

Judas' embrace was really a signal, showing the soldiers which man to seize and arrest.

Jesus is Taken Away

At first, Jesus' disciples tried to put up a fight. One of the Bible stories says that Peter grabbed his sword and attacked the men who were arresting Jesus. The story says that he cut off an ear from the head of the high priest's servant. But Jesus did not want the servant to suffer, so he healed the cut immediately.

Jesus did not offer any resistance himself. When his disciples saw it was hopeless they ran away, just as Jesus had told them they would.

As Jesus was marched off to the home of the high priest, only Peter dared to follow. Although he could not go inside with Jesus, Peter waited about in the courtyard to see what would happen. He was frightened for himself as well as for Jesus. Three times that night, curious servants asked Peter if he was one of Jesus' disciples. Three times the terrified man said he was not.

Only days earlier, Jerusalem had welcomed Jesus as a king. Now the city's leading men treated him as if he was a murderer.

The Crucifixion

Jesus had always told people to be loving towards one another. Now some of the very men he had taught would kill him with great cruelty.

His enemies had planned it with care. They had seized him at night when there were few people about to rescue him. Next day they took him to Pilate, the Roman governor, the only man with power to sentence anyone to death.

Pilate gazed hard at the pale young prisoner before him. Jesus looked so pure and noble that Pilate found it hard to believe he could be blamed for anything deserving the death penalty. As far as Pilate knew, Jesus' only crime had been to annoy Jews by claiming to be their king.

At last Pilate asked Jesus, "Are you the king of the Jews?"

Jesus gave a puzzling reply, "My kingdom is not of this world."

After more questions Pilate took Jesus before a waiting mob, and said "I find no fault in him."

But when he offered to release Jesus (Pilate freed one prisoner at Passover time each year) the crowd yelled, "Not this man. Free Barabbas!" (Barabbas was a robber.) So Pilate had Jesus whipped, and crowned with thorns. Pilate hoped all this would satisfy the mob.

But the mob cried, "Our law says liars who called themselves the son of God must die. Crucify him!"

Pilate knew his job meant keeping peace in Palestine at any cost—even executing innocent men. So he unhappily agreed that Jesus should be hung from a giant wooden cross until he died. It was a common way of executing criminals.

Jesus was forced to walk out to the hill of execution carrying the heavy cross on his back, though a kind stranger called Simon of Cyrene helped him. Then men cruelly nailed his wrists to the wooden arms of the cross, and raised it upright. Above Jesus' head someone fastened a sign that read: *The King of the Jews.*

On the Cross

For hours, Jesus hung on the cross tormented by his enemies.

"Look at you now!" they jeered. "If you're who you say, why don't you save yourself and come down?"

Jesus' pain-filled gaze wandered over the crowd who had come to watch him and the two thieves crucified beside him. Suddenly he noticed his mother Mary. She was standing near Jesus' disciple John, and crying. Jesus told John to take her home and be like a son to her.

As Jesus grew weaker the sky darkened and the ground trembled. Men who had jeered grew afraid that he really had been God's son, and this was God's way of showing his anger at what they had done.

Suddenly Jesus cried out, "Father, I give my spirit into your care! It is finished." Then he died.

The Resurrection

Perhaps the most astonishing of all Bible tales are those about what happened after Jesus died.

No one doubted he had died—a soldier made sure of it by jabbing a spear in Jesus' side as he hung on the cross. That night, friends secretly took his body, wrapped it in a scented cloth and laid it in a tomb, shut by a huge stone.

Then, on Sunday morning, two days later, extraordinary things began to happen.

When Jesus' follower Mary Magdalene visited the tomb, she found to her surprise that the door lay open. She was horrified to find no corpse inside. Mary wept to think that anyone should steal her teacher's body. Then, through her tears, she glimpsed two angels sitting in the tomb where Jesus had been lying.

Just then she heard a voice and turned to see a man behind her.

"Why do you cry?" he asked. "Who are you looking for?"

Blinking at him through her tears, she thought she saw a gardener.

"If you have taken him away", she sobbed, "please tell me where he is."

The man just said, "Mary!" and suddenly she knew it was Jesus—the dead Jesus, but standing there as much alive as she was! Imagine her amazement and delight.

Doubting Thomas

Mary Magdalene was only the first to see Jesus risen from the dead. That night, the Bible says, he appeared to his disciples as they met secretly behind locked doors. It was as if he walked through the wall, as ghosts are said to do. Indeed, the disciple called Thomas doubted that the real Jesus had been there at all. But then Thomas only heard about the visit later, for he had spent that evening somewhere else.

The next time Jesus showed himself, he proved that he was real by making Thomas feel the scars left by the crucifixion—scars where nails had pierced his wrists and the soldier's spear had gashed his side.

Jesus by the Sea of Galilee

Jesus appeared to his disciples at least once more. But things were never quite as they had been before he died. Now he never stayed for long, and sometimes they did not even recognize him at first.

It was like this when seven of them had been fishing on the Sea of Galilee. They had rowed around all night throwing out their nets, without landing a single fish.

As dawn broke a man standing on the beach called out, "Any luck?"

"No!" they shouted back.

Then he cried, "Throw the net on the right-hand side of the boat. You'll find plenty there."

They did—and he was right! When they hauled the net ashore, scores of big, juicy fishes were flopping helplessly inside.

John knew this was no ordinary luck. Realizing who the man must be, he shouted. "It's the Lord!"

Jesus stayed for breakfast. His last message to his followers was this: "Go out into the world and tell everyone the good news that I bring. Those who believe, and are baptized, will be saved."

Jesus' work on Earth was over, and the Bible says that when he finished speaking, his disciples saw him taken up into heaven.

Now it was up to them to carry on the task he had begun.

The Stoning of Stephen

Jesus used to warn his followers that enemies would beat and torture them for what they preached. He said that some of them would even die because of their beliefs.

People who perish in that way are known as martyrs. Since Jesus Christ himself hung on a cross about two thousand years ago, thousands of his followers have met a martyr's death. The first of them was a young Jew called Stephen.

Stephen had earned a special place among Jerusalem's early Christians (as Christ's followers became known). For he was not just deeply religious; he was clever too. Christian leaders made Stephen one of seven deacons, with the job of caring for the Christian poor.

But Stephen became best known for preaching powerful sermons, and for cleverly defending his Christian faith in arguments.

One day, a group of Jewish leaders tried to prove to Stephen that he was wrong when he preached that Jesus was the son of God. But Stephen's answers were so wise that his opponents found they had no arguments left.

So, instead, they plotted an excuse to have him put to death.

First, they paid some men to tell lies about Stephen. This made people hate him, and led the Jewish leaders to arrest him and have him brought before their council. As Stephen faced his judges and accusers he guessed how horribly his trial would end. But he listened calmly as lying witnesses accused him of cursing God and Moses. Any Jew found guilty of such charges was likely to be sentenced to die.

The judges watched Stephen closely to see how he reacted. To their surprise, instead of looking angry or ashamed, his face seemed to glow with glory like an angel's.

The high priest was so astonished that he felt Stephen deserved at least a chance to defend himself. So he asked, "Did you really say these dreadful things?"

Stephen's Defence
The Jewish leader soon wished he had not invited Stephen to speak, for once he began he seemed to talk for hours. Stephen reminded everyone of the history of the Jews from the time of Abraham onwards. Then he told how, one after another, rulers had ignored God's voice and killed his prophets.

Stephen finished by saying, "You are just as bad as they were, for you killed Jesus—God's savior sent to Earth to help mankind."

The longer Stephen talked, the more angry the Jewish leaders became.

At the end he could almost hear them grind their teeth with rage.

Stephen knew they felt furious because he had shown *they* were the truly guilty ones. He also knew nothing he could say would affect the court's verdict.

Yet this knowledge only made him braver. Gazing up into the sky he said, "I see Jesus standing next to God in heaven."

It was the last straw. Until then Stephen's enemies had kept fairly quiet. Now they shouted him down, and clapped their hands over their ears to shut out the sound of Stephen's voice.

In fact there was no verdict. The court became a mob that dragged him out, rushed him through narrow streets, past the city gate, and down a stony track.

The First Martyr

Stephen knew his end was near as the mob left him standing alone, while they began to search the ground for chunks of rock.

Moments later they began to hurl hard stones at Stephen's defenceless body. Stephen was soon knocked down. Bruised and bleeding, he still found strength to cry out, "Lord, forgive them!"

Stephen remembered, in his own agony, that Jesus had said this very prayer for those who had nailed him to the cross.

Soon afterwards Stephen was knocked unconscious, and died.

On the Road to Damascus

No one hated Christians more bitterly than a young man called Saul. Yet one day Saul would want to make the whole world believe in Jesus' Christian teachings. This story from the Bible tells how he changed his mind.

Young Saul believed that all the Christians were wicked, because they claimed that their leader, Jesus, was the son of God. Saul felt this must be untrue, and anyone who said it deserved the very harshest of punishments for such a terrible lie.

In fact, Saul gladly looked after the heavy cloaks thrown off by other Jews, when they stoned the first Christian martyr, Stephen, to death.

Later on, Saul did his best to crush all the Christians in Jerusalem. He rushed from house to house, hauling Christian men and women off to jail

and execution. Hundreds of Christians fled from the city, but Saul was determined to track them down. So, when he heard that some of them had traveled to Damascus, he set off with troops to drag them back in chains.

Saul didn't guess that this trip would change his life for ever.

The Dazzling Light

After a long, hot journey over mountains and dusty deserts, Saul had almost reached Damascus. Now he paused on a hilltop, and gazed down at the plain before him. After all that rock and dust it was pleasant to see green fields, olive groves and vineyards. And there, shimmering in the sunlight, rose the walls and towers of the lovely city.

But Saul's smile turned to a frown, as he remembered that his task was catching Christians.

Just then, the bright sunlight seemed to grow still brighter. In a moment the travelers found themselves bathed in a flash of light so dazzling that it almost seemed to burn through their eyes.

Saul glanced up—and fell back, blinded. As he lay on the ground, bewildered, he heard a strange voice. It was not one of his companions speaking, and the voice seemed to echo in his head. It said, "Saul, Saul, why do you persecute me?"

Saul realised the voice must come from God. "Who are you, Lord?" he asked.

"I am Jesus", came the answer.

Then the voice continued, "Go into the city, and you will be told what to do." At once, Saul felt that the Christians were right and he had been wrong; Jesus *was* the son of God.

Saul's Eyes Are Healed

The light faded, the voice disappeared, and Saul struggled to his feet. His companions saw that he had lost his sight and so they led him to Damascus. Here he lay for three days without food or drink. He thought of the voice he had heard, and he seemed to hear it again, telling him that a Christian would come and heal his eyes.

Meanwhile, news of Saul's arrival had reached the Christians of Damascus, and they were terrified. But one of them, called Ananias, had a strange dream. Jesus came to him and told him to help Saul. So, although Ananias knew only too well what Saul could do to him, he went to where Saul was staying.

"Jesus has sent me to you", said Ananias. "He wants you to be a Christian." And he laid his hands gently on Saul's eyes. Immediately, Saul could see again! Minutes later, Saul was baptized.

From then on Saul was a different man. He made friends with the people he had once hated, and he preached Christian ideas in the Jewish temples. Everyone who heard him was astounded. "Isn't this the man who used to try to destroy the Christians?" they asked.

Paul's Travels

Paul—as Saul was later called—became a great traveler, and he took Christian teachings to lands far beyond Palestine. In those days long-distance travel could be risky, and Paul was shipwrecked three times.

Perhaps his most dangerous voyage was his last and longest. This was to the west, to Italy. As a Roman citizen Paul went to stand trial in Rome, wrongly accused of making trouble elsewhere in the Roman Empire.

Paul and 300 others set sail from Egypt in a big, square-sailed grain ship. At first all went smoothly. Then an autumn gale sprang up and the ship began drifting helplessly through mountainous waves.

Passengers and crew began to panic. Then, above the roar of the

storm, they heard Paul call out calmly, "Take courage! An angel of God has told me that we shall all be saved. Only the ship will be lost."

That helped to quieten them. But day after day the storm still drove them before it. Everyone was too scared to eat properly, until Paul set them an example.

At last the water grew shallow, and a sandy shore loomed up through the spray. The crew raised the mainsail and the ship raced for the beach. But soon it ran aground, and began breaking up.

Soldiers, prisoners, merchants, crew—everyone had to swim for their lives. But, just as Paul promised, all landed safely on what turned out to be the island of Malta.

Paul was now frail, old and soon to die. But he had achieved his life's work—the task of spreading Jesus' message far and wide.

Index